You are children
of God.

♡ - Tiffany

ISBN 978-1-64300-500-3 (Paperback)
ISBN 978-1-64300-501-0 (Hardcover)
ISBN 978-1-64300-502-7 (Digital)

Covenant Books, Inc.
11661 Hwy 707
Murrells Inlet, SC 29576
www.covenantbooks.com

# Which Way Is It to Heaven?

### Tiffany M. Campione

# A Message to Parents

Thank you for taking time to read this book to your amazing children! My prayer is that it will encourage the next generation to read their Bible daily. God can transform the intimidation we occasionally feel, for an indescribable love of His Word. When I made the decision to read the Bible daily a few years ago, it changed my life forever and has become my mission to share the Good News with others.

As parents, raising our children has its challenges, but God is gracious and gave us His Word to guide us through every season. I would love to join in community with you to discuss daily devotions, Bible studies, parenting tips, philanthropic opportunities, and more. I appreciate your feedback and would be happy to answer any questions you have. You can follow me on Instagram @tiffanymcampione or email me at tiffanymcampione@gmail.com

I'm so thankful we are on this journey together.

With love,
Tiffany

Train a child in the way he should go, and when he is old he will not turn from it — Proverbs 22:6

*To my greatest gifts from Heaven,*

*Sophia and Gianna,*

*Thank you for showing me a glimpse of Heaven each day and for inspiring me to write this book. It was through your curiosity that God placed this story on my heart. I pray you both will always keep your eyes fixed on Heaven and trust He will lead you well. Remember, when this world brings you trouble turn to the One who calls you chosen, beloved child.*

"Which way is it to Heaven, Mama?" spoke a voice so small.

"That's a very important question, I'm so glad you asked, my child."

"This place called Heaven I've heard so much about. I want to see it for myself. Oh please, won't you tell me how?"

"Slow down my child. No need to rush, for you have so much life to live. Just keep your eyes fixed on Heaven, and one day you will see."

"Mama, what if I fly the fastest airplane and peek through the clouds in the sky or blast off in a rocket ship and zoom past the stars in the night?"

"*There will be times on your journey you will feel like you are floating on the softest cloud in the sky. Breathe in these moments of God's sweet grace and place them in your memory bank.*"

"Can I climb Mount Everest or swim through the Caribbean Sea? Then will I be there, Mama. Then will I finally see?"

When you pass through the waters I will be with you.

Isaiah 43:2
NIV

"This life at times will feel like you are climbing a steep mountainside, but God will be right there with you as you ride in on the evening tide."

6

"What if I take a roller coaster up and down and all around? Will that bring me there, Mama? Oh, please won't you tell me?"

"Just like your favorite roller coaster, you will move through life's twists and turns. At times you will smile bright, while others you may be scared. "But don't worry my love, this is all a part of growing your faith as you journey to Heaven's Gate."

Proverbs 3:5

Trust in the Lord with all your heart and lean not on your own understanding

8

"Is there a map to Heaven Mama, that will show me the way?"

"Well actually yes, there is a map to guide you to Heaven's gate. Right here my darling, this will teach you the way."

The child looked at the book while curiosity danced across her beautiful face.

"The Bible, my dear this is your map. It will keep you from wandering and help if you ever feel lost. For the way to Heaven is written on these pages. Open it and you will see that Jesus is the way to Heaven. It's God's promise to all who believe."

*"Just remember to always be kind, my love, to everyone that you meet. And when you see those in need, give to them as He has given to you and me."*

*"On earth we must shine our light, my darling, wherever we may go so that others will see God's love through us and then their light will glow. That day we are called to Heaven, I pray will be a long time from now, but until then my angel just look around."*

The Lord is my shepherd
He gives me everything
I need.

Psalm 23:1 NIRV

13

*"God has sprinkled pieces of Heaven right here for us to see. I feel Heaven in your sweet snuggles my love, and in the warm sunshine."*

# The heavens declare the glory of God;

"I see it in your joyful smile and in the twinkling night sky. I feel it when I hold your hand and when we pray at night. I see it when you learn how to do something for the very first time."

he skies proclaim the work of his hands

Psalm 19:1

16

*Pleasant words are a honeycomb*

*Sweet to the soul and healing to the bones*

Psalm 16:24

"We taste Heaven in the sweetness of honey and feel it here in the breeze. I look at you, my sweet child, and see a little glimpse of Heaven right before me.

"I think I can feel Heaven Mama, every day when you play with me! And at nighttime when we sing our songs and when you kiss my cheek."

"That's right, my love. The love we feel is Heaven on earth, and for now, that's all we need."

I
am
the
way

and
the
truth
and
the
life.

John 14:16

18

# About the Author

Tiffany Campione is excited to share her first children's book with the world. This story was inspired by her children and a whisper from God to go for it. Raising her daughters has been her greatest accomplishment. Instilling faith, confidence, and truth into their lives is a gift. Until recently they served alongside her husband as a military family. Over the years, uprooting their family taught them that home isn't a place; it is where love surrounds you.

Tiffany has published several faith-based articles, substitute teaches at her children's school, and creates hand-stamped jewelry.

Her favorite way to spend the weekend is hiking with her family, watching Hallmark movies, and baking with her girls while dancing in the kitchen.

To learn more about upcoming book signings and events follow @tiffanymcampione on Instagram or email her at tiffanymcampione@gmail.com

CPSIA information can be obtained
at www.ICGtesting.com
Printed in the USA
LVHW072004221119
638214LV00003B/13/P

9 781643 005010